The Boy Who Cried Wolf

A Tale About Telling the Truth

Retold by Joanne Barkan
Illustrated by Gary Undercuffler

Famous Fables™

Reader's Digest Young Families

Long ago, in a faraway land, a kind shepherd lived with his son, Julian. Every day at dawn, they led their flock of sheep up to a grassy meadow near the woods. They watched over the sheep all day. At sunset, they led them back to their little farm.

One evening the shepherd said, "My brother is sick, and I must go to him right away. I'll be gone for three days. You've never taken care of the flock by yourself, so I'll ask someone from the village to help you."

"I don't need any help, Father," Julian said with confidence. "I know exactly what to do."

The next morning, Julian said good-bye to his father and led the flock up to the meadow.

At first Julian enjoyed being in the meadow
alone. He lay under an oak tree, daydreaming.
But by mid-afternoon, he was bored.

"There's no one to talk to," Julian said to himself.
"Everyone is down in the village. How can I get
someone up here to keep me company?"

Then Julian had an idea. "I'll shout 'wolf' as loud as I can. When the villagers come running to help me save the flock, I'll say it was a joke. We will all have a good laugh."

Julian stood at the edge of the meadow. He shouted down to the village, "Wolf! Help! Wolf!" He shouted again and again.

Julian chuckled as he watched the villagers run toward the meadow. Some carried pitchforks or shovels to scare away the wolf.

When they reached the meadow, Julian said, "There's no wolf. I was just having some fun."

"Fun!" one woman said. "We don't have time for your kind of fun, Julian. We have work to do."

The villagers grumbled angrily as they left the meadow. But Julian was still enjoying his joke.

The next day, Julian led his sheep back to the meadow. He lay under the oak tree and watched the clouds drift by. By noon, he was feeling very lonely.

"I wish Father were here," he said to himself. "I miss him so much."

The hours slipped by. Julian felt more and more alone. Finally, he couldn't stand it anymore. He jumped up. Without thinking, he began to shout, "Help! A real wolf! Help!"

Again the villagers rushed to the meadow. Again they found there was no wolf. This time they were even angrier.

"Julian," they said, "don't bother us again!"

On the third day, Julian sat under the oak tree and watched his flock. The hours went by slowly. In the late afternoon, he heard a noise in the woods. He turned around to see who was there.

A pair of yellow eyes stared back at Julian. A pair of pointed gray ears twitched.

"A wolf!" Julian screamed. He ran to the edge of the meadow. "Wolf! Wolf! Help me! I'm telling the truth this time!"

The wolf leaped out of the woods. Its body was long and muscular. Its large jaws were open wide.

"*Baaaa. Baaaa,*" cried the sheep fearfully. They began running in all directions. Julian shouted for help again and again.

No one came.

Julian watched helplessly as the sheep fled from the meadow. The wolf chased them until they were scattered all across the countryside.

Frightened and upset, Julian waited until sunset. But the sheep didn't return to the meadow. He was about to go back to the village when he saw someone hurrying toward him.

"Father!" he shouted. "The sheep are gone!"

The shepherd looked at his son sternly. "Our neighbors told me that you shouted 'wolf' when there was no wolf."

"That was yesterday and the day before," Julian said. "But today there really was a wolf, and no one came to help me. The sheep ran away!"

"Julian," his father said slowly, "always remember this. If you tell lies, no one will believe you when you tell the truth."

Julian's eyes filled with tears. He nodded and said, "I understand now."

When they got back to the village, Julian went to each of his neighbors and apologized. All the next day, he and his father searched for their sheep and found them one by one. Julian never cried wolf again—unless he was telling the truth.

Famous Fables, Lasting Virtues
Tips for Parents

Now that you've read The Boy Who Cried Wolf, *use these pages as a guide to teach your child the virtues in the story. By talking about the story and its message and engaging in the suggested activities, you can help your child develop good judgment and a strong moral character.*

About Telling the Truth

Just about all young children sometimes make up stories to hide the truth or tell an outright lie. Like Julian, they may do it for attention. Or they may do it to please their parents about something. Or they may be dishonest in order to avoid getting into trouble. It's upsetting for parents when their children don't tell the truth, especially when the evidence is obvious (your child may deny he ate the candy while looking at you with chocolate on his face). It's important to know that many children younger than seven or eight years old often have trouble distinguishing the difference between fact and fiction. This is normal. But it's never too early to begin teaching the importance of telling the truth. Here are some ideas:

1. *Show that it's safe to tell the truth.* Your child probably understands the difference between your disapproval of misbehavior and your approval of being truthful about it. If your child misbehaves but is honest about it, the consequences should be less than if he misbehaves and lies. When childhood infractions occur, try your utmost not to react too strongly — even if you are exasperated, exhausted, or extremely angry in the moment. Strong consequences in such situations may cause a child to be afraid to acknowledge wrongdoings for fear of punishment and may, ironically, lead to even more untruths.

2. *Reinforce your family's rules.* Avoid questions that accuse your child of misbehavior—such as "Did you hit your brother?" — especially when the answer is already obvious to you. These kinds of questions often lead to defensiveness and untruths. Instead, try to react matter-of-factly and address the misbehavior by restating your family's rules: "Hitting is not acceptable in our family" or "We don't eat candy before dinner." If your child does tell a lie, restate the rule about honesty: "We always tell the truth in our family."